Ever After High™

BY ROYAL DECREE...

Little, Brown and Company

Hachette Book Group
237 Park Avenue, New York, NY 10017
Visit our website at lb-kids.com

Little, Brown and Company is a division of Hachette Book Group, Inc.
The Little, Brown name and logo are trademarks of Hachette Book Group, Inc.

The publisher is not responsible for websites (or their content) that are not owned by the publisher.

First Edition: August 2014

Library of Congress Control Number: 2013948839

ISBN 978-0-316-28359-5

10 9 8 7 6 5 4 3 2 1

WOR

Printed in the United States of America

Ever After High™

THE SLEEPOVER SPELLEBRATION
PARTY PLANNER

Hexcellent!
I love a party!

By Kirsten Mayer

LITTLE, BROWN AND COMPANY
NEW YORK BOSTON

Once upon a Time...There was Ever After High – a b...
children of fairytale legends learned to relive their...
to or not.
That is until R...
everything...

A Royal DECREE

YOU KNOW THE SLEEPING BEAUTY STORY: PRICK YOUR FINGER AND SLEEP FOR ONE HUNDRED YEARS. BUT IF YOU SNOOZE, YOU LOSE!

Briar Beauty knows her destiny is to take the big nap, so in the meantime, she's going to live life to the fullest. And that means that any reason is a good reason to have a party! Her favorite type of party? A sleepover! (She usually doesn't do much sleeping, though!)

Briar knows the main ingredients for an enchanting soiree are friends, food, and fun! This planner will help you organize your own sleepover worthy of the royal seal from the party princess!

Briar's first tip: If you want to throw the most enchanted sleepover party the village has ever seen, you've got to start at the beginning of the story—with the king or queen of the castle! Talk to your parents or guardian and get permission to have a sleepover!

Now it's time to choose your

party destiny!

What story will you write for your

spellebration?

CHOICE CHECKLIST

- ○ Theme
- ○ Date
- ○ Guest List
- ○ Invitation Style
- ○ Decorations

- ○ Snacks
- ○ Muse-ic
- ○ Activities
- ○ Goodie Baskets

Theme Time

Apple White likes to keep things organized, so she starts planning early and makes lots of lists. Before you can plan a party, you need a theme!

Do you want to spellebrate something special or just enjoy the current chapter with your BFFAs (best friends forever after)?

Having a theme will help you work out all your party details, down to your decorations, party favors, snacks—even your music playlist!

Some past party themes from Ever After High:

BOOK TO SCHOOL PARTY

NATIONAL ROSE DAY

LEGACY DAY BASH

TRUE HEARTS DAY

Brainstorm more ideas here:

Make a Choice

MY PARTY THEME IS:

PARTY COLORS:
any color

First, Date

Now it's time to start planning your spellebration. Look at the royal calendar and decide which might be the best day to have your party. If it's during the Ever After High school year, you might want to pick a Friday or Saturday. But if it's over Chapter Break, you can hold it during the week!

Make a Choice

THE DATE OF MY SLEEPOVER PARTY IS:

MY PARTY WILL START AT

MY PARTY WILL END AT _____ THE NEXT MORNING.

I WILL ASK GUESTS TO BRING

GUESTS NEED TO RSVP BY _____ .

Guesting Game

Raven knows that the most important part of any event is having your friends there. You won't be able to fit the entire cast of characters in your house, so you'll have to narrow down the guest list to a handful of your BFFAs. Feeling a little rebel? Invite one new friend into the mix!

Use this space to work on finalizing your list.

Make a Choice

Now collect your guests' contact information for sending out your invitations. Also, make a note of any food allergies or requests your friends might have. Not everyone likes porridge!

Guest: _____

E-mail address: _____

Mailing address: _____

Special food requests: _____

Guest: _____

E-mail address: _____

Mailing address: _____

Special food requests: _____

Guest: _____

E-mail address: _____

Mailing address: _____

Special food requests: _____

Guest: _____

E-mail address: _____

Mailing address: _____

Special food requests: _____

Guest: _____

E-mail address: _____

Mailing address: _____

Special food requests: _____

Guest: _____

E-mail address: _____

Mailing address: _____

Special food requests: _____

Guest: _____

E-mail address: _____

Mailing address: _____

Special food requests: _____

Guest: _____

E-mail address: _____

Mailing address: _____

Special food requests: _____

Rock 'n' Royal
Invitations

It's time to create your invitations! You can choose to make them by hand and mail them to all your BFFAs, or you might take a more high-tech approach and e-mail out an invite you designed. Briar and her friends all have different styles. Steal some of their ideas for your party invitation looks.

Briar dabs some rose-scented perfume on her invitations!

Raven glues studs and rhinestones to her invites and then hand-delivers them.

Apple prefers sending invites from her MirrorPhone—she embeds a tune from a songbird with the invitation.

Maddie loves to sprinkle loose tea in the envelopes like potpourri!

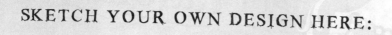
SKETCH YOUR OWN DESIGN HERE:

To:

From:

You're Invited!

Where:

When:

Dress code: Royal or Rebel

R S V P by:

Decadent Decorations

Decide which room you will have most of the party in—your bedroom or the living room? Then make the place look spellbinding with these decorating ideas!

Pillow Presents

Everyone knows a sleepover requires lots and lots of pillows to lounge around on—and to have pillow fights with! Pile every pillow in the house in the party room. Use pillowcases of different colors—especially if you have red and purple. For an extra royal touch, tie a ribbon in a bow around each pillow.

Royal Room Redo

Want a more hextreme makeover? Add special touches around your bedroom to mirror Briar's and Raven's rooms at Ever After High! Use sheets or other fabric to create a canopy over your bed like Briar's, or fill a table with battery-operated candles like what Raven has beside her bed.

BRIAR'S DORM ROOM

RAVEN'S DORM ROOM

Rose-a-Palooza

Briar thinks roses are the most hextastic flower. You can put real roses in containers around the room (Maddie likes to put them in teacups or mugs), or plan to make your own flowers with your friends! Homemade ones can be decorations, accessories, and keepsakes! Try these enchanting craft ideas:

Ribbon Roses

RIBBON

SCISSORS

TAPE

Cut a two-foot-long strip of fabric ribbon about half an inch wide. Lay the ribbon out flat, then fold at the halfway point so it looks like two sides of a square.

Alternate folding each ribbon half over the other until you have a stack of folded ribbon and an inch left.

When you release the folds, it will look a little like an accordion.

Hold one ribbon end firmly while you—slowly and gently—pull on the other ribbon end to magically form a rose!

Carefully tape or staple the ribbon ends together to secure.

Paper Roses

CREPE PAPER STREAMER

- Start with a strip of crepe paper streamer.
- Roll one end into a flower "center" that you can hold on to.
- Slowly wind the streamer around the center, crinkling and gathering the bottom edge into the center, letting the top edge fan out as the "petals."

- When the flower is big enough, wrap a green pipe cleaner around the bottom to secure the flower and make a stem!

Riddlish Ribbon Place Settings

Maddie knows from working in her dad's Haberdashery & Tea Shoppe that even the smallest touches can make a guest feel special. Personalized place settings are fun and easy, and they double as party favors!

Charming Cups

Buy plastic or paper cups in your party colors, or in Royal red and Rebel purple. Then:

- Decorate the cups by tying ribbons around them and writing your friends' names on them with markers or metallic pens. Glue on some rhinestones!
- As an alternative, you can also buy cute paper labels at an office supply store, write your friends' names on the labels, and then stick them onto the cups.

Part of the decor is how you set your table!

Spellbinding Silverware

Buy plastic silverware in your party colors, or in Royal red and Rebel purple. Here are some ideas to decorate forks, knives, and spoons for your guests:

- Tie ribbons around the handles.
- Inscribe a guest's first initial on each handle with a metallic marker.
- Coat the handles in glue and dip them into glitter.
- Glue rhinestones to the handles for a bejeweled look.

Table Service

Tie each silverware set together with a ribbon and a flower, and place it in the cup to set the table!

Page-Ripping Party Snacks!

To keep everyone's energy up for a real page ripper of a party, you need to plan a menu. Here are some ideas!

BRIAR BEAUTY'S SPICE-OF-LIFE POPCORN

Briar loves to try new things, like HeXtreme Games sports and hextreme flavors. Pop some popcorn and sprinkle it with different toppings for a royal treat! Try a spice like paprika, or even Parmesan cheese!

WRITE SOME IDEAS FOR POPCORN TOPPINGS HERE

Make a Choice

APPLE WHITE'S CHOCOLATE APPLE BITES

Apple loves any treat with her favorite fruit,
like apple crumb cake or these easy-peasy
bites. Have an adult help you melt some
white chocolate chips in the microwave.
Then dip apple slices halfway and let
them cool on a plate.

APPLE SLICES

plus

WHITE CHOCOLATE

RAVEN QUEEN'S PRINCESS AND THE PEA-NUT BUTTER MINI SANDWICHES

Raven once played a little prank on her roomie, Apple, by hiding a green pea under her mattress to see if she'd notice, as a true princess would! Make peanut butter and jelly sandwiches with your favorite jelly and then use your cookie cutters to cut out mini sandwiches in cute shapes! Hide a peanut (it's yummier than a pea!) in one sandwich to see which princess finds the "pea"! Set out the rest of the peanuts in a snack bowl!

Royal Hint

You can also make the sandwiches with just jelly and hide a berry in one sandwich if one of your BFFAs is allergic to peanuts.

MADELINE HATTER'S PARTY PUNCH

Set out an array of juices and sodas, a bucket of ice, and a few flavors of sorbet. Your guests can mix together their own concoction and top it off with a small scoop of sorbet for a fizzy drink!

PUNCH

plus

SORBET

Breakfast Feast

Don't forget—you have to serve a royally magical breakfast the morning ever after your sleepover spellebration! Ashlynn likes to start the day off right!

PANCAKE BAR

Set out some special toppings, and then let your guests turn an ordinary breakfast into a scrumptious treat! Use toppings like these, and come up with more on your own!

- whipped cream
- cinnamon sugar
- red and purple sprinkles
- chocolate chips
- syrup
- chocolate syrup
- cheese
- apple slices
- peanut butter
- marshmallows

Make a Choice

_____

_____

_____

_____

_____

_____

SPARKLING ORANGE JUICE

For an easy and fanciful breakfast drink, pour one-third sparkling water with two-thirds orange juice, and put a raspberry in each glass. Try this with other juices, too! Grape juice would be a rebellious option! Destined to be delicious!

Spinmaster Flax Dance Party

Set aside an hour for a totally hexcellent dance party! Go in the yard or push back the furniture in a room so you have lots of space to dance. Plug in your playlist and jam! Plan for a punch break afterward—you'll be thirsty!

Briar's DJ alter ego is Spinmaster Flax. (Shhh! It's a secret.) Play DJ yourself and make a playlist ahead of time so you can just let the music play! Write down your songs here:

Make a Choice

_____

_____

_____

_____

_____

_____

_____

Raven's Rave Review
Film Fest

No sleepover is complete without watching a charming movie. Make a list here of potential ones to watch and have them ready. When the time comes, let your guests vote on which movie to watch! Serve some Spice-of-Life Popcorn and enjoy!

Make a Choice

Apple White's Fairytale Theater

Apple starred in all her spellementary school theater productions, and now she loves to play charades. Write the title of each fairytale listed on the right on separate slips of paper. Fold each slip and place it in a large bowl or basket. Split into two teams, Royals and Rebels. A member from one team draws a piece of paper out of the bowl, looks at it secretly, and then acts it out in silence for her team. No narrating! The actress can't give any clues out loud. Use a timer to give the actress forty-five seconds. If the team guesses the fairytale correctly, it scores a point. Then the other team takes a turn, and so on! See which team can guess the most tales!

Are you a Royal or a REBEL?

26

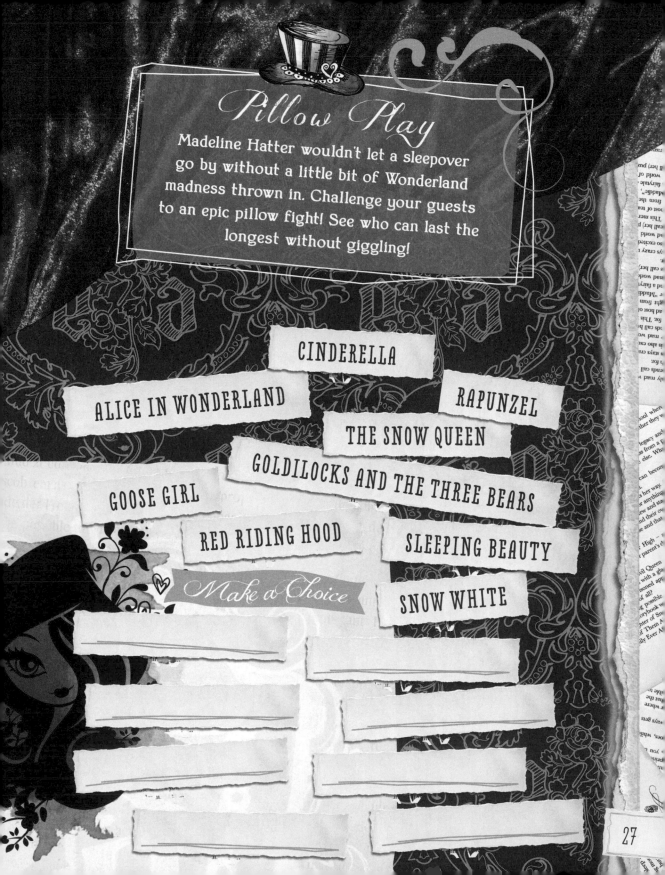

Pillow Play

Madeline Hatter wouldn't let a sleepover go by without a little bit of Wonderland madness thrown in. Challenge your guests to an epic pillow fight! See who can last the longest without giggling!

CINDERELLA

ALICE IN WONDERLAND

RAPUNZEL

THE SNOW QUEEN

GOLDILOCKS AND THE THREE BEARS

GOOSE GIRL

RED RIDING HOOD

SLEEPING BEAUTY

Make a Choice

SNOW WHITE

Royal or Rebel Says

Instead of Truth or Dare, play a game of Royal or Rebel Says! Everyone takes a turn—when it's your turn, choose Royal or Rebel and your BFFAs will select one of the challenges on the right for you to perform! There's room for you to think up more tasks!

Totally SPELLBOUND

Royal

Hexcellent

REBEL

DARE TO Wonder

Royal Says

- Bestow an honorary title on everyone in the room. Invent names such as Lady Cupcake or Frosting Cake Downs.

- Give a speech about the importance of woodland creatures.

- Walk like a princess—walk across the room with a book balanced on your head.

Make a Choice

Rebel Says

- Have your friends yell out "left" or "right" and try to raise the *opposite* hand.

- Attempt a cartwheel with just one hand.

- Eat dessert first! Stuff as many marshmallows into your mouth as you can.

Make a Choice

Destiny Dreams

Give each BFFA a piece of paper and ask her to write down her name and what she'd like her destiny to be—at least for today! (You can always rewrite your destiny tomorrow.) Collect the papers (or ask an adult to do that if you want to play, too!). Read each destiny out loud and have everyone guess who wrote it!

EVER AFTER HIGH

My Destiny:

Royal Hint

Record all the destinies in the back of this book and then reread them in a month and see if anyone followed their destiny!

List Service

Every rose has its thorn and every Royal has a little Rebel inside. Make a sheet of paper for each guest with her name written at the top. Divide each sheet into two columns and write *Rebel* at the top of one column and *Royal* at the top of the other. Leave the sheets out during the party and let your guests know that they should go and write down a totally Royal and totally Rebel thing about each person. In the morning, your guests can see what everyone wrote!

EVER AFTER HIGH
Royal

EVER AFTER HIGH
REBEL

Apple White

ROYAL	REBEL
Kindness to all	*Wants to run her own kingdom*

Goodie Baskets

Before the party, have a little going-away present set aside for each of your guests to thank them for coming. Cerise Hood is the best at arranging packets full of treats for her friends. Buy small baskets at a craft store and tie ribbons around the handles, or decorate paper bags with custom name labels, metallic markers, and more.

Get creative!

Make a Choice

Now, what will you put inside?

Here are some ideas to get you started and space to come up with your own:

- a book you love to read
- stickers
- nail polish
- a journal
- a quill pen

Briar Beauty's
Marshmallow Pillow Pops!

Briar takes her pillow purse with her wherever she goes, just in case she needs a quick nap. She loves to take these adorable treats with her, too—in case she needs a quick *snack*! They are also the perfect treat for your sleepover goodie baskets!

SUPPLIES:

LARGE MARSHMALLOWS

LOLLIPOP STICKS FROM A BAKING-SUPPLY STORE

A BAG OF CHOCOLATE CHIPS, WHITE CHOCOLATE, OR SOME OTHER MELTABLE CANDY CHIP

SILVER SPRINKLES OR COLORED SUGAR

HOW-TO:

1. Push the end of a lollipop stick firmly into the center of a marshmallow—but not all the way through. Then put the sticks in the freezer for a few minutes to help firm up the marshmallows and keep the sticks in place.

2. Put the chips into a microwavable bowl and microwave the bowl thirty seconds at a time until the chips are melted. Stir every thirty seconds to keep the melted chips smooth.

3. Gently dip the marshmallows partway into the melted chips to coat the top half. Let any excess drip off.

4. Have the sprinkles or sugar ready in a small bowl or on a plate. You can either dip the marshmallow into one of them to coat it more thoroughly, or use your fingers to just sprinkle a little bit on top.

5. Once you've decorated your marshmallows, stand them up in a narrow glass or jar, and let them set in the refrigerator for at least half an hour.

Tip: Ginger Breadhouse loves to decorate with food! Tie the Marshmallow Pillow Pop onto a gift bag or basket with a ribbon, or create a fun centerpiece for the breakfast table by covering a piece of Styrofoam or florist foam with something pretty and sticking the pops into the foam!

Don't forget to include a thank-you note! Here's an example from Raven:

Dear _____,

Thank you so much for taking the time to attend my spellebration. It was also so hexcellent that you helped me clean up after the party. I really didn't mean to spill the party punch— I was trying to add some fizz with a spell! Oh well!

I hope we have another reason to spellebrate soon!

Crown wishes,

_____

The End

The Morning Ever After

Ashlynn Ella loves how pretty the house looks after it's been cleaned up! A-tisket, a-tasket, trash goes in the wastebasket! Ask all your BFFAs to help you play the role of Cinderella. Throw out any trash, take the bedding to the laundry room, put away the pillows, and wash everyone's silverware before breakfast.

Destined To-Do List!

Apple White knows that running a kingdom someday means she needs to know how to organize and plan big events. She always likes to start with a Destined To-Do list. Write your own on these pages!

Make a Choice

The

your happily

Decoration Shopping List!

W rite down all the craft supplies you need to make decorations for the party!

Make a Choice

ribbons

metallic markers

glitter

Dreams

Ribbon Roses

TAPE

RIBBON

Party Snack Shopping List!

Write down all the food items and ingredients you need to stock up on before the party!

Make a Choice

juice

popcorn

pancake mix

SHOPPING
LIST FOR

Pillow Pops

LARGE
MARSHMALLOWS

LOLLIPOP STICKS FROM
A BAKING-SUPPLY STORE

SILVER
SPRINKLES OR
COLORED SUGAR

A BAG OF CHOCOLATE CHIPS,
WHITE CHOCOLATE, OR SOME
OTHER MELTABLE CANDY CHIP

Rock 'n' Royal
Invitation Templates

P**hotocopy these design ideas for your invitations!**

You're Invited!

to a SLEEPOVER SPELLEBRATION

Date:

Time:

Place:

EVER AFTER Royals!

Photocopy these design ideas for your invitations!

Raven Queen
SLEEPOVER
SPELLEBRATION

Date

Time

Place

You're Invited
to a SLEEPOVER SPELLEBRATION

Date:

Place:

Time:

I love going to sleepover spellebrations with my fairy best friends!

47

Sleepover Spellebration Memories

Dreams

Re-write Your Happily Ever After

Ever After High

Ever After Starts Now

Destiny

48

Ever After Hig